For
Mum, Dad and Nan

Published in 1995 by Magi Publications
55 Crowland Avenue, Hayes, Middx UB3 4JP

© Jo Moore, 1995

Printed and bound in China
Produced by Mandarin Offset

ISBN 1 85430 260 4

Jo Moore

Timmy

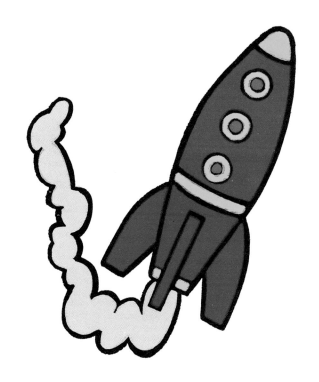

MAGI PUBLICATIONS
London

TRRRING, TRRRING!
What's the time . . . ?

Time to get up.
Here I come!

HA, HA, HA!
Guess what I am . . . ?

Timmy the clown,
making you laugh.
HEE, HEE, HEE!

BRRM, BRRM!
Guess what I am . . . ?

Timmy the racing driver,
whizzing past.
VROOM, VROOM!

GRRRR, GRRRR!
Guess what I am . . . ?

Timmy the monster,
looking for my lunch.
MUNCH, MUNCH!

ABRACADABRA!
Guess what I am . . . ?

Timmy the magician,
waving my wand.
HEY PRESTO!

5..4..3..2..1, BLAST OFF!
Guess what I am . . . ?

Timmy the spacecat,
going to the stars.
WHOOOSSH!

YO, HO, HO!
Guess what I am . . . ?

Timmy the pirate,
sailing the seven seas.
LAND AHOY!

TICK, TOCK!
What's the time . . . ?

Time for bed,
ZZZZZZZ . . .